Tales from
ADVENTURE
TIME

THE UNTAMED SCOUNDREL

by T. T. MacDangereuse

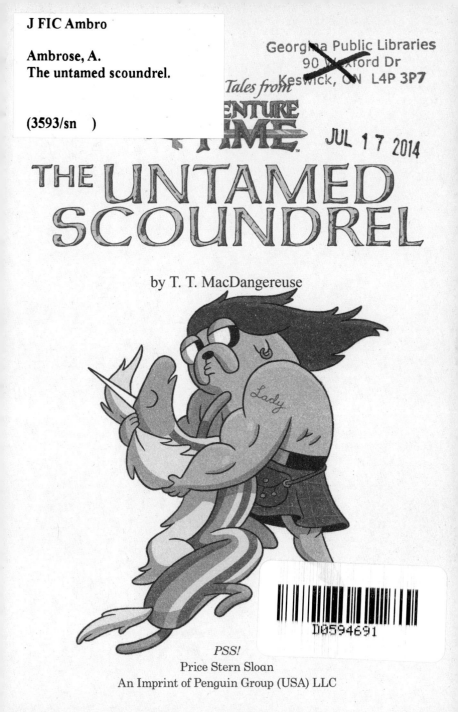

PSS!
Price Stern Sloan
An Imprint of Penguin Group (USA) LLC

PRICE STERN SLOAN
Published by the Penguin Group
Penguin Group (USA) LLC, 375 Hudson Street, New York, New York 10014, USA

USA | Canada | UK | Ireland | Australia | New Zealand | India | South Africa |
China

penguin.com
A Penguin Random House Company

Published in 2014 by Price Stern Sloan, a division of Penguin Young Readers
Group, 345 Hudson Street, New York, New York 10014. *PSS!* is a registered
trademark of Penguin Group (USA) LLC. Printed in the USA.

Text written by Adrianne Ambrose
Cover illustrated by Christopher Houghton

ISBN 978-0-8431-8032-9   10 9 8 7 6 5 4 3 2 1

Greetings, fans of epic adventure . . .

What you are holding in your hands is one of the most amazing novels in all of Ooo. These fantastical adventures by the master of awesome storytelling, T. T. MacDangereuse, are filled with tales of unimaginable heroism, perilous wonder, and unspeakable marvel. While some of these characters may seem familiar to you, keep in mind that nothing is what it seems when you enter the mind of T. T. MacDangereuse.

CHAPTER 1

Lady Gooddog sat glaring at her only son across the breakfast table. "What did you do to Lumpy Space Princess on your picnic yesterday?" she demanded, her voice echoing off the tall ceiling of the dining hall.

"Nothing," Sir Jacobus said with a shrug of his broad shoulders, his muscles rippling under his luxurious golden fur.

"You had to have done something," Lord Gooddog insisted as he helped himself to another large slice of apple breakfast pie.

"I didn't. I swear," Sir Jacobus said, sounding a little defensive. "All I did was eat the sandwiches she made, and then drink the apple juice she'd squeezed, and then take a nap on the blanket that she quilted to celebrate the picnic. After that, Finn and I went to check out the barrel races, which were totally rad." Mr. Finnish Biped, aka Finn, was Sir Jacobus's Hu-manservant. He was known throughout the Kingdom of Plaid for his love of battle and his great loyalty to his lordship, and best friend, Sir Jacobus.

Lady Gooddog shook her head, her eyes raised toward the ceiling. "I can't believe how insensitive you are."

Her son was confused. "It was just a picnic. What's the big deal?"

"The big deal," thundered Lord Gooddog, "is that Lumpy Space Princess was expecting you to propose."

"Propose?" Sir Jacobus sputtered. He had been taking a large swig of apple cider, and his father's comment caught him by such surprise that a bit of the juice sprayed out his nose. "But she's all lumpy," he managed to say after he'd stopped coughing.

"And space princessy," Finn added from where he lounged in a chair, using a toothpick to pry a piece of apple skin out from between his teeth.

Lady Gooddog fixed the servant with an angry glare. "Mr. Biped, do you really think it's appropriate for a servant to sit at the breakfast table with his master's family? Is that what servants do?"

"I don't know," was Finn's reply. "It's what I do and I'm a servant, so yeah, I guess it kind of is."

The lady gave a resigned sigh. "Could you at least take your feet off the table?" she asked.

"Yeah, Finn," Sir Jacobus told him. "That's really gross and some of us are still trying to eat."

"Fine," his manservant said, thumping his feet onto the floor. He reached across the table to help himself to another apple.

Turning back to her son, Lady Gooddog continued with, "Did you ever stop to think why Lumpy Space

Princess went to all that trouble for your picnic?"

"Not really," Sir Jacobus admitted as he finished his apple porridge. "I just figured she likes to do that kind of stuff."

"I don't think you realize how upset the princess really is," his father told him. "She's been on a shopping tirade since yesterday afternoon. All the shop clerks throughout the kingdom have been terrorized." He cocked an ear toward the window. "Listen, I think I can still hear her now."

Everyone was quiet for a moment. It wasn't too difficult to hear the voice of Lumpy Space Princess echoing across the land. "You call that pink?" she roared. "That's, like, totally mauve at best. How dare you try to tell me that mauve is pink! Do you know who I am?"

Then there was another voice, a frightened male voice. It was obvious that he was doing everything within his power to be conciliatory. "I am so sorry,

Miss Lumpy Space. It must be the lighting in here. I sincerely thought it was pink. Let me go and fetch you a pink one from the back."

"That's Lumpy Space Princess to you! I am royalty!" she informed him. There was a loud bang and the sound of glass shattering.

"Oh. Is that what that is?" Sir Jacobus said, scratching his head. "I heard that when I got up this morning, but I thought the kingdom was just infested with dragons again."

"Oh, too bad," Finn said, looking a little disappointed. "I love fighting dragons. That would have been totally math."

Lumpy Space Princess wasn't finished yet. Her tirade continued. They could hear her yelling, "No, I don't want a different size. It's not my job to fit into your stupid clothes. It's your job to design fashion around me."

Sir Jacobus gave his father a penetrating look.

"Are you sure that's not dragons?"

"Yes, I'm sure," Lord Gooddog said, getting a bit hot under his frilled collar. "Listen, Jacobus. This has got to stop. You've broken the heart of almost every maiden in all of Plaid. People are starting to talk. When are you going to choose a wife?"

"A wife?" Sir Jacobus said, a little shocked. "Why would I want a wife? I'm a scoundrel."

"An untamed scoundrel," Finn added, putting his feet back up on the table as he happily munched on the apple.

"It's true," the only child of Lord and Lady Gooddog said with a prideful grin. "No one can tame me."

"Well, you listen here, Mr. Untamed Scoundrel," Lady Gooddog said, getting to her feet and slapping Finn's shoes off the table. "At tomorrow night's ball, you are going to choose a bride. Do you hear me? Because if you don't, you are going to be a very poor untamed scoundrel." Her son was about to protest, but she cut him off. "Either you choose a bride at the ball, or your father and I will disown you and cut you off without a cent."

"Aw, man," Sir Jacobus said. "You guys wouldn't do that, would you?"

"We've already put the wheels in motion," Lord Gooddog said, getting to his feet to stand at his wife's side. They faced their son as a united front. "We sent out an announcement first thing this morning, telling all eligible female guests that it is your intent to choose a bride at the ball."

"What the zip? This really stinks," Sir Jacobus said, crossing his arms over his broad chest. "How the heck am I supposed to do that?"

"I don't know," his mother told him, "but you'd better figure something out by tomorrow evening."

"This really ducks," Sir Jacobus grumbled as he slouched out of the dining hall with his Finn at his side. "What's the point of being an untamed scoundrel if I'm married?"

"Yeah, dude," Finn agreed. "You'd be, like, totally tamed."

"Maybe I should just tell my parents that they can keep their old fortune," Sir Jacobus said, sounding a little sulky. "I mean, I don't really care about the money as long as I can keep living in the castle and have nice clothes and fine food and plenty of servants to do all my stuff for me."

"Yeah," Finn said, pursing his lips a little, "I'm pretty sure they mean you're not going to be able to have any of that stuff, either."

"Doggone it!" Sir Jacobus said with a huff. "Well, I don't think I'd like being poor, so I guess I have to let somebody tame me." He let his broad shoulders sag. "But how am I supposed to choose a bride by tomorrow night?"

"I know!" Finn said, brightening. "I have a plan

that is totally amazing. It will make sure you get the coolest and most awesomest bride ever."

"What?" the Gooddog asked, looking up eagerly. He knew his Hu-manservant and best friend wouldn't let him down.

"We'll hold a tournament. And the girls can compete. With, like, jousting and stuff. And whoever wins the tournament will obviously be supercool, so that's how you'll know who to marry," Finn explained.

"That's a great idea!" Sir Jacobus agreed. "I mean, not the jousting because Mom doesn't like it when I bring horses in the castle. The last time we tried that she totally yelled. But we should definitely have a tournament."

"Okay, cool," Finn said with a smile. "I'll put out an official proclamation letting the ladies know they should come to the ball ready to rumble."

CHAPTER 2

The next evening, Sir Jacobus stood in the ballroom wearing his best kilt and his royal purple sash. His fur had been brushed until it was glossy and smooth. He was eagerly awaiting the arrival of the guests for the ball. "I wonder if any of the ladies will come dressed in armor," he said, rubbing his paws together in anticipation. "That would be so awesome. I'm totally excited."

"I know," Finn agreed. His black uniform had been starched and pressed to perfection. "I can't wait until the womenfolk start battling it out. Winner take all."

Sir Jacobus smiled. "This is going to be awesome." His heart began beating a little faster as he heard the first carriage pull up outside the castle door. He'd never been so keen for a ball to begin in his life.

"Princess Bubble of Gum," a footman announced as the first guest arrived.

"That's Bubblegum," the princess corrected him as she made her entrance. Her pink gown was two parts perfection and one part confection; the dress was like a swirling mound of cotton candy that highlighted Princess Bubblegum's long pink hair, which was piled in cascading curls on the top of her head. She was the ruler of the Candy Kingdom, and she looked every bit the part.

"Why are you dressed like that?" Sir Jacobus asked as he walked up to greet her.

"What do you mean?" she asked, looking down at her gown. "This is a ball, isn't it?"

"Yeah, but I was hoping you'd at least come dressed like a ninja," he told her, wrinkling his nose at all the pink.

"Why would I do that?" the princess wanted to know.

"Because you were supposed to come dressed for battle," Finn interjected. "You're not going to be able to fight very well in that." He made a disgusted face at the delicate pink frills.

"I don't intend to fight at all," the princess informed them, smoothing her hands over her skirt.

"Didn't you get Sir Jacobus's message about how there's going to be a tournament to see who gets to marry him?" the Hu-manservant asked, sounding surprised. "I know I delivered a note to your palace. I gave it to the Peppermint Butler. He swore he'd give it to you."

"Oh yeah," Princess Bubblegum said. "That." She shook her head. "I'm not doing that."

"Why not?" Sir Jacobus asked, feeling a little hurt. He was, after all, exceedingly rich and handsome. It seemed like the kind of combination girls usually liked.

"Because it's degrading to expect that women would be willing to fight each other over you," she said, giving him a stern look. "And besides, don't you always brag about being an unashamed scoundrel?"

"That's untamed scoundrel," Sir Jacobus said, correcting her.

"Either way," Princess Bubblegum replied, patting her perfect pink hair. "I'm not interested in competing."

"That's because you know you're gonna lose," said a voice from across the room.

"Lumpy Space Princess," the footman announced, but the Lumpy Space Princess already was floating toward them. She still looked like a lumpy, bumpy purple cloud, but she had attached a veil to her head. "I look totally hot and I'm ready to dominate at this tournament thingy," she informed them. "Don't you think I look awesome, Sir Jacobus?"

"Yes, you look very . . . um . . . lumpy," he finally said.

"And space princessy," Finn added.

"I'm totally going to win," Lumpy Space Princess said, floating way too close to Princess Bubblegum and forcing her to take a step backward to avoid a collision.

"I so do not want to marry Lumpy Space Princess," Sir Jacobus said in a strained whisper to Finn. "The Lumpy Space Princess is all lumpy."

"And space princessy," Bubblegum added, even though his comment wasn't directed at her.

"Don't worry," Finn assured him. "No one's even here yet. I'm sure there will be dozens of beautiful young women willing to fight it out so they can be married to you. I mean, come on, you're Sir Jacobus Gooddog."

"You'd better be right," Sir Jacobus grumbled.

More and more guests kept arriving for the ball, and more and more young women were dressed in beautiful gowns. None were dressed like knights or ninjas. No one wanted to compete in the tournament.

"This is awful," Sir Jacobus said, covering his face with his paws. "Why did I let you talk me into this?"

"It's going to be all right, man," Finn said, patting him on the back. "All the guests aren't here yet. There's still a chance that someone totally hot might want to compete. Listen," he said, cocking an ear toward the door. "I think another carriage just arrived."

"Tournament!" a voice could be heard bellowing over the crowd.

"Miss Susan Strong," the footman announced before hopping quickly out of the way of the giant woman who had just entered the room. He was, after all, just a foot.

"Tournament!" Susan shouted again, swinging a big club through the air and forcing several of the other guests to duck. She was in a gown like the rest of the female guests, but still wore her kitty-cat hat.

"You totally need to back off!" Lumpy Space

Princess shouted, hurrying across the ballroom. "I am winning this tournament unopposed."

"Tournament!" Susan yelled, happily thwacking the princess with her knobby club.

Lumpy Space Princess ricocheted off the ceiling, skidded off the snack table, and ended up flipping the punch bowl, splashing dozens of the guests with fruity refreshment. "Hey!" someone from the crowd said in an indignant voice. "My dress is ruined. This stain will never come out. It's silk."

"Deal with it," was Lumpy Space Princess's response. Then she turned to stare down Susan. "Oh no you dih-un't," Lumpy Space Princess said, brushing bits of artichoke dip off her veil. Before anyone could do anything to stop her, she was rushing toward the giantess again.

"I guess the tournament has started," Finn said, wearing a big grin. "This might turn out better than we thought."

As Lumpy Space Princess barreled down on her opponent, Susan raised her club and started swinging. "Lumpy!" she said, quite happily making contact with the princess again. "Lumpy, lumpy, lumpy."

"And space princessy," Princess Bubblegum was heard to say from somewhere in the crowd.

"Ow, you're hurting me," Lumpy Space Princess whined, trying to flee the giantess. "That's totally not fair."

"Lumpy!" was Susan's reply, taking another swing. She missed her enemy, but managed to send a Gumdrop from the Candy Kingdom sailing out the window.

"I had a lovely time. Thank you for inviting me!" the Gumdrop called as she disappeared from view.

"Now wait just a minute," Princess Bubblegum said, making her way through the astonished crowd. "You've got no call to be clubbing my subjects. That Gumdrop never did a thing to you."

"Lumpy!" Susan Strong pronounced, feeling the weight of her club in her hand and smiling menacingly.

"Are you calling me lumpy?" Princess Bubblegum wanted to know, narrowing her eyes and putting her hands on her hips.

"It's an honor," Lumpy Space Princess informed her, keeping a safe distance from the reach of the club. "She's totally complimenting you."

"Lumpy," the giant said again, this time without as much conviction. There was an unexpected fierceness in this new opponent's eyes that Susan hadn't encountered with her first challenger.

"This is a disaster," Sir Jacobus said to his Hu-manservant. "I don't want to marry Susan, either. And there's no way Princess Bubblegum can beat her. Do something."

Thinking fast, Finn raised his voice to be heard over the crowd. "Ladies and gentlemen, the Tournament for Love is about to begin."

Susan Strong raised her club, ready to squash Princess Bubblegum with one mighty swing.

Panicking, Finn blurted as quickly as possible, "The use of outside weapons leads to automatic disqualification." Then he added, directly to Miss Strong, "Sorry, Susan. You're out."

"Awww," Susan moaned in a sad voice, dropping her club to the ground. "I make good bride."

"Yay! I win," Lumpy Space Princess said, throwing her hands in the air.

"Uh, no you don't," Finn told her. "Where did you get that idea?"

"Because I'm the only other contestant," she explained. "And my wedding is going to be the most awesomest wedding anyone has ever seen. And I am going to have a beautiful dress and tons of bridesmaids and a caramel fountain and instead of rice, everyone is going to throw white chocolate chips and . . ."

"So we're going to start registering contestants

now," Finn said, talking over Lumpy Space Princess while desperately scanning the crowd for anyone who looked at all willing to compete.

"It's too late," Lumpy Space Princess insisted. "No one's interested. Sir Jacobus, you just need to start falling in love with me right now."

"It's not too late," Finn told her. "The tournament is just starting."

"Whatever," Lumpy Space Princess said, rolling her eyes. "I'm totally going to win, anyway."

"Who wants to sign up?" Sir Jacobus asked, feeling a bit desperate. "Anyone? Anyone?"

CHAPTER 3

"Count me in," Princess Bubblegum said, stepping forward. "I'll compete in your stupid tournament thingy."

"You will, PB?" Sir Jacobus was surprised. "I thought you said having women compete to marry a man was degrading and you would never participate?"

"Yeah, well that was before someone splashed punch all over my dress." She whirled around to confront Lumpy Space Princess. "Do you know how many cotton-candy trees it took to make this gown?"

"Whatever," was Lumpy Space Princess's reply as she folded her arms and showed PB her back. "It wasn't that nice, anyway. I'm totally hotter."

"Yeah, I'll sign up, too," Flame Princess said, stepping forward.

"You want to marry me?" Sir Jacobus asked, a little surprised. Flame Princess was pretty hot.

"Not particularly," she admitted, "but I got splashed with punch, too, and it dowsed half my dress. I'm super furious about it." Her fiery hair got even fierier as she spoke, and her eyes glowed as red as hot coals. "And I'm ready to throw down."

More girls stepped forward, eager to fight. Most of them were pretty mad about their gowns being ruined. No one mentioned anything about marrying the son of Lord and Lady Gooddog.

"Good thing Lumpy Space Princess made a big splash with that punch bowl," Finn said in a quiet voice. "Otherwise, I think you'd be in a lot of trouble."

"You don't have to tell me," Sir Jacobus replied.

By the time they got everyone registered, there were about two dozen females ready to duke it out. "The first event is a licorice tug-of-war," Finn announced to the gathering.

"What kind of licorice is it?" Flame Princess asked, sounding a bit suspicious.

"I don't know," Finn had to admit. "The regular kind."

"Because red licorice isn't really licorice," the princess informed him.

"Yeah, it has to have essence of the licorice root to be licorice," Princess Bubblegum agreed.

"So, what color is it?" Lumpy Space Princess asked. "Red would go better with my outfit, but I want to keep it real."

"Does it matter?" Sir Jacobus couldn't help but snap. "It's still a tug-of-war."

"Okay, fine," Flame Princess said sullenly. "I was just asking."

The contestants were divided into two teams,

and a long, thick rope of black licorice was stretched between them. An enormous cream pie was set in the middle of the room. "Whichever team pulls the other team into the pie first wins," Finn informed the contestants.

"Does that mean all of the winners will marry Sir Jacobus?" Princess Bubblegum asked. "Because that sounds kind of creepo to me."

"No, this is just the first event," the Hu-manservant assured her. "There will be lots of opportunities to win Sir Jacobus's love."

"Oh goodie," PB said, rolling her eyes to emphasize the sarcasm.

"Okay, ladies," Finn called, raising his voice so everyone could hear. "When I drop this red flag, then you need to start pulling. Ready? Set." He dropped the flag. "Pull!"

Both teams of females began hauling on the wide rope of licorice, but almost instantly there was a loud *snap* and everyone fell backward. "Whoops!" Finn said, smacking his hand to his forehead. "Who knew licorice wasn't that strong?"

"What should we do with the giant cream pie?" a footman asked, hopping forward.

"Save it for later," he was told by Finn. "I'm sure we can think of something to do with it."

"Okay, well . . . that was a giant waste of time," Flame Princess said, her hair becoming more fiery.

"Better announce the next event quick," Sir Jacobus whispered in Finn's ear. "I think the ladies are getting a bit annoyed."

"Moving right along," Finn said while raising his hands in the air to draw the contestants' attention. "For the next event in the Tournament of Love, we have the gumball shot put."

"What's that?" Princess Bubblegum asked, not sounding at all enthusiastic.

"I had these special gumballs made up," Finn

explained, rolling out a large green ball that was as big as a dinner plate. "All you've got to do is throw your gumball farther than anyone else and you're the winner of the event."

The females lined up and selected their gumballs. "I need a purple one," Lumpy Space Princess insisted. "There's no way I'm throwing anything that doesn't go with my outfit."

"Good luck with that," Flame Princess told her. A couple of the other competitors snickered.

"Why . . . you . . ." Lumpy Space Princess flung her purple gumball at Flame Princess. She missed by a mile, but the gumball bounced off the marble floor of the ballroom and crashed through a stained-glass window.

"My window!" Lady Gooddog shouted. "That was over two hundred years old."

"Sorry," Lumpy Space Princess called as she hurried to hide behind the crowd.

"No you don't," Flame Princess said, flinging her own gumball at the other princess and nearly taking down a chandelier.

"Stop it! Stop it this instant!" shouted Lady Gooddog. "No more throwing gumballs. This event is over. Put your gumballs down immediately." The girls did as they were told. Sir Jacobus might have been an unapologetic scoundrel, but his mother had always treated them very nicely and they had no desire to upset her.

"Better move on quickly," Sir Jacobus told Finn. "And make it something less destructive. Mom might blow her stack if anything else gets damaged."

"Okay, okay, okay," Finn said, holding his hands in the air again. "Moving on to the next contest, we're going to have a marshmallow bounce," he announced.

"Oh great. What the heck is that?" Flame Princess growled. Several of the contestants could be seen grumbling or rolling their eyes.

Finn did his best to ignore the discontent. "Each of you will be given one large marshmallow." He gestured toward a pile of stool-size fluffy white treats. "And you'll use it to bounce across the ballroom. The first one to cross the finish line wins this event." Marshmallows were soft, so Finn figured no one could do too much damage to the castle. Lady Gooddog was still not looking very pleased.

"But what if I already am a Marshmallow?" pointed out a guest from the Candy Kingdom who was fluffy, white, and looked absolutely scrumptious.

"Oh," Finn exclaimed. He hadn't factored in that many of the guests were actually Candy People when he made up the competition. "Um . . . well . . . just do the best you can."

The contestants lined up at one end of the room, with their marshmallows beneath them. "Ready? Set. Bounce!" Finn shouted, pulling the ripcord on a party favor and sending confetti shooting into the air.

The girls started bouncing as fast as they could. And the marshmallows proved to be extremely springy. "Ouch!" a Why-wolf exclaimed as she bounced so high she bumped the ceiling. "Why would you make us do this? Why?"

"My marshmallow's melting," Flame Princess complained as the fluffy confection sagged beneath her. "This contest is rigged for creatures that aren't made out of fire."

"Whatever," Lumpy Space Princess said as she bounced past. "I'm totally going to win, anyway. It's my destiny."

"*Grrr!*" Flame Princess roared, shooting a blast of fire after the other princess and scorching Lumpy Space Princess's marshmallow. The next time LSP tried to bounce, her marshmallow stuck to the floor with a splat.

"You're totally cheat—*gah!*" Lumpy Space Princess shrieked as another contestant was unable to stop bouncing and piled into the back of her.

"Look out!" the Marshmallow on the marshmallow shrieked as she too got caught in the pileup. And then more girls fell over her, causing complete chaos.

"Who won?" Sir Jacobus asked, making his legs extralong so he could peek over the pile of princesses and assorted gentlewomen.

Finn tried climbing to the top of the marshmallow-covered girls to look over the other side to the finish line. "I can't tell."

"Ouch! Get off!" someone shouted from the pile.

"Oh, the humanity!" wailed the Marshmallow. "I can't tell where I stop and another marshmallow begins."

"Oops," Finn said, shaking his head as he looked at the gooey marshmallow madness. "Maybe we should just call it a draw and move on to the next event?"

"Forget it," Princess Bubblegum said as she

extracted herself from the sticky pile. Her cotton-candy gown was completely ruined. She turned to face the females, who were all looking pretty fed up. "Girls, I say we stop putting up with this nonsense. Why are we letting these boys be in charge?"

"Yeah! Stop the madness! Just say no," several voices called from the pileup.

"So, what are we going to do about it?" Princess Bubblegum demanded.

"Coup d'etat! Coup d'etat! Coup d'etat!" the girls all started chanting, pumping their fists in the air.

"What are they shouting?" Sir Jacobus asked. "And why are they shouting it?"

"Um, it's an expression in some weird language, but I think it means that they are going to overthrow the tournament officials and set up their own rules," Finn said as he jumped down from the pile.

"They can't do that," Sir Jacobus said, shrinking his legs back to their normal size. "What if they try to be fair about things and I end up with someone that I don't even like?"

"Yeah, it's just like girls to try to be fair about stuff," Finn agreed. "What are we going to do?"

Sir Jacobus folded his arms and glared at his Hu-manservant. "Well, this was your idea. Think of something. Quick!"

"I know," Finn said, brightening with fresh inspiration. He raised his voice above the crowd. "Ladies, please, I have an announcement."

CHAPTER 4

"Ladies," Finn said again, in a louder voice. The crowd was pretty feisty, but they quieted down a little to listen. "I'm sorry the first few events haven't worked out so well."

"That's an understatement," a voice said from the crowd.

"Well, to make everything fair," he went on, "plus the fact that we've only got the caterers until midnight, we're going to settle the Tournament of Love with one final competition. Winner take all!"

The room fell completely silent. The girls all stared at Finn with stony expressions.

"Okay, I'll bite," Princess Bubblegum finally said after several long moments. "What's this competition? And it better not be dirtballs."

"It's not," Finn insisted, but he was looking a little nervous. "What's going to happen is all of you are going to form a big circle. And you can arm yourselves with anything you want. But it has to be food. So, like, cupcakes or candy corn or pies or whatever. And then, when I give the signal, you all start throwing the food at each other."

"You want us to do what?" asked a small Cupcake, who was barely taller than Finn's knee.

"Food fight!" Finn shouted, pumping his fist into the air.

Princess Bubblegum walked up very close to Finn, leaned over, and poked him on the chest a few times while asking, "Are you trying to promote Candy-on-Candy violence?"

"Of course not," the Hu-manservant insisted. "No

throwing friends or family. Obviously. What's wrong with you, Princess Bubblegum? Why would you even ask me that?"

"Why are we being asked to do this again?" the Why-wolf wondered aloud.

"This is stupid," the Marshmallow agreed. "I'm not doing this. I barely know who I am anymore."

"That's because you're a quitter," Lumpy Space Princess said, picking up the Marshmallow and chucking her across the room.

"Hey!" Princess Bubblegum shouted. "You shouldn't have done that."

"Why not?" Lumpy Space Princess asked, folding her arms and glaring at the other princess. "You're all a bunch of losers. I'm the only winner here."

"Why would you say such a thing?" the Why-wolf asked, looking rather offended.

"Because she's an insecure little brat," Princess Bubblegum growled.

"You can't say that about me!" Lumpy Space Princess said. She floated over to the snack table, picked up a tart, and flung it at Princess Bubblegum.

"Missed!" Princess Bubblegum crowed, after quickly ducking to one side. The Penguin standing behind her was not so lucky.

"Finn, I don't know about this food fight idea," Sir Jacobus said. "Maybe we'd better . . . *guuhhhh* . . ."

Frowning, Finn turned to look at his master. "Huh?" Sir Jacobus looked weird. Like, really weird. "What's wrong with you, dude?"

"Who is that?" Sir Jacobus whispered, his heart pounding in and out of his chest like a cuckoo bird popping out of a clock.

"Who?" Finn asked, looking around.

"Over there," Sir Jacobus said, trying to appear casual, although his eyes were as big as saucers. "The most beautiful creature in the room."

"Which room?" Finn asked, not sure if his boss

was looking into another dimension or something.

"Who is that beautiful creature with the rainbow skin and the horn in the middle of her head?" Sir Jacobus asked, pressing his paw to his chest to stop his heart from pounding so loudly. "She's breathtaking."

"Oh!" Finn said, finally figuring it out. "That's Lady Rainicorn. She's a rainicorn."

"Lady Rainicorn," Sir Jacobus whispered, and the words felt like music when he spoke them. "Who did she come with? Why haven't I been introduced?"

"I don't know, dude," Finn said with a shrug. "She's been around. It's kind of hard to miss a rainbow-colored horse with a horn in the middle of her forehead."

Turning to his servant, Sir Jacobus said, "Tell the band to strike up a waltz. I'm going to ask the lady to dance."

Finn shook his head. "I don't think it's going to be that easy, dude."

"Why not?" Sir Jacobus asked, the pupils of his

eyes turning into the shape of Valentine's hearts. A fruit pie sailed right past his left ear and he didn't even notice, he was so enchanted with the lovely lady.

"See that girl dressed all in black standing next to her?" Finn asked, pointing across the room.

"Yeah. She's cute and all," the Gooddog said, "but she's nothing compared to Lady Rainicorn."

"Well, I'm pretty sure I remember hearing she's a witch. And if you're hanging around with a witch all the time, it probably means you're under some kind of evil spell or something," Finn explained. "I bet that witch doesn't let you anywhere near Lady Rainicorn."

"That's stupid." Sir Jacobus waved a dismissive paw at his servant. "I'm going to ask Lady Rainicorn to dance." He made it two steps before he slipped on a slice of Bundt cake.

"See," Finn said. "The witch probably zapped that up. I don't even think we're serving Bundt cake at this party."

"Well, then you've got to distract the witch somehow and give me a chance," Sir Jacobus told him as a sprinkle of jelly beans bounced off his head.

"Like what?" Finn asked. "I'm not going to start a fire or anything, just because you've got a crush."

"Are you insane?" Sir Jacobus gave him a concerned look. "I'm not asking you to start a fire. Just go sing her a song or ask her to dance or something. Go charm her."

"Charm her?" Finn grumbled to himself as he walked across the room, nearly slipping on a smashed cupcake on the floor. First he headed over to the band. "It's waltz time," he told the bandleader. "And make it romantic."

"Are you sure?" asked the bandleader, who was a tall Peppermint Stick with a snazzy bow tie. "The female guests seem to be a little riled. I'm starting to fear for the band's safety."

"Don't be such a wimp," Finn called over his

shoulder as he turned to initiate his romantic assault on the witch. "Everything's going to be fine."

"Javelin!" Miss Susan Strong yelled as she charged the bandstand, snatching the bandleader off his post.

"Play 'The Waltz of the Flower' in D," the Peppermint Stick instructed his bandmates as he was flung through the air toward several females fighting over a baguette.

"Hey there, witchy-poo," Finn said, sliding up to the girl dressed all in black. He held out his hand. "What do you say you and I take a spin on the dance floor?" There was a smattering of candy corn that rained down on them, which he ignored.

"Witchy-poo is close, but actually my name is Marceline," she corrected him.

"I'm Finn. Let's hit the floor and groove," he told her, spinning in a circle and then holding his hand out to her again. A pizza went sailing across the room like a Frisbee and splattered on the wall next to him.

The musicians started playing the waltz. It didn't really sound like groove music. "Nah, that's okay," Marceline said. "I told Lady Rainicorn I'd stick with her. But thanks for asking."

"I knew it," Finn said to himself.

"What's that?" the witch asked.

"Oh...um...nothing." Finn could see Sir Jacobus sneaking behind the witch's back as he approached Lady Rainicorn. The Hu-manservant knew he had to keep the witch distracted. "Awww, come on, baby. Cut Lady Rainicorn some slack. Maybe she wants to get her groove on, too."

"Excuse me," Marceline interrupted him, "but she doesn't need any slack. And why do you keep talking like that?"

"Like what?" Finn asked, caught by surprise as a cream puff came whistling through the air and bounced off his knee.

"Why do you keep using weird slang? Is there something wrong with you?" she wanted to know, giving him a penetrating look.

"No," he insisted. "I just thought girls liked it when guys were all confident and charming and stuff."

"We do like confidence," Marceline had to admit. "But I'm not sure how you're acting is actually considered charming." She ducked as several dinner rolls flew past.

"Really?" Finn scratched his head. "So, what is charming?" He really wasn't all that interested either way, but if he could keep the witch talking, that would leave more time for his good buddy to romance Lady Rainicorn.

As Sir Jacobus crossed the room, much to his surprise, his knees began to tremble. Then he was there, standing in front of the most beautiful creature he had ever beheld, Lady Rainicorn. The heir to the Gooddog estates had stood next to many females, dozens of them being considered reasonably attractive by one species or another, but none of them had done anything to his knees. None of the ladies had made them tremble. That's how he knew that Lady Rainicorn was the girl he'd been waiting for. It was all in the knees. He cleared his throat, feeling overly nervous. "Excuse me," he said, and then cleared his throat again. The room was getting quite noisy.

Lady Rainicorn turned to look at him. Her eyes were like limpid pools of water, her breath as sweet as summer hay, her mane as glossy as unwoven silk. "네?" she asked, batting her large eyes, her long eyelashes swishing through the air.

"I was wondering . . . ," Sir Jacobus managed to stammer out, "if . . ."

"Food fight!!!" Miss Susan Strong shouted.

Instantly, it was as if they were on the deck of a ship during a storm, but instead of being lashed with water, they were slammed with noodles in a light cream sauce. Jelly beans fell like hail—brightly colored, painful hail.

The female guests had all simultaneously unleashed their inner frat boys and decided to trash whatever delicious morsels the caterers had provided. "Stop!" Lumpy Space Princess wailed. "It's not supposed to be like this. You're supposed to be fighting each other, not throwing things at me." No one listened to her as a raspberry pie slammed her in the face.

"Lady!" Marceline shouted, throwing her arms over her head to shield herself from another onslaught of jelly beans. "We've got to get out of here."

Lady Rainicorn was immediately by the witch's side, moving like a flowing ribbon. The witch leaped onto her back and then the two of them disappeared out the window. Finn and Sir Jacobus ran to the opening and looked out just in time to see Marceline riding the beautiful Rainicorn across the sky. They quickly disappeared into the night.

"That proves it," Sir Jacobus said with a gasp. "My fairest love is under the spell of that evil witch."

"You think?" Finn asked with a bit of a frown.

"Sure," his master told him. "Why else would they have left in such a hurry?" A pie slammed into the back of Sir Jacobus's head. "What was that?" he asked his friend.

Finn leaned over to take a look. "Looks like banana cream." Large scoops of mashed potatoes slapped against their bodies in rapid fire. "This food fight is turning into a bit of a disaster," the Hu-manservant observed.

"Yes," Sir Jacobus Gooddog had to agree, "but I consider the evening a success because I have found true love."

CHAPTER 5

"I absolutely forbid it!" Lord Gooddog thundered, slamming his paw onto the table, causing the breakfast china to jump.

"It's ridiculous," Lady Gooddog agreed. It was the next morning, and she was still a bit rattled from the previous night's out-of-control festivities. "A Gooddog with a Rainicorn? Our grandchildren would have hooves."

Sir Jacobus clenched his fists at his sides. "You're the ones that told me I had to choose someone from the ball. And I did."

"You did say that," Finn said, happily munching

on an apple, his feet propped up on the dining table.

"Yes, but we meant someone like Princess Bubblegum," Lady Gooddog insisted, shoving the Hu-manservant's feet onto the floor. "We would have even been willing to welcome Lumpy Space Princess into our family if that was the way your heart led you. But this . . ."

"My heart led me to Lady Rainicorn and, as my parents, you're just going to have to deal with it," Sir Jacobus insisted, folding his arms over his manly chest.

"But, son, we have our position as a family to think about," his father tried to explain. "Gooddogs are Gooddogs, and Rainicorns are Rainicorns, after all. There is just no compromising."

"Too bad," Sir Jacobus said with a growl. "You said I had to choose and she's the one I've chosen."

"Well, choose again," Lord Gooddog insisted. "We're not going to let you throw yourself away on a

Rainicorn. We'd disown you first."

"Disown me?" Sir Jacobus narrowed his eyes at his mom and dad. "You're bluffing," he told them. "Go ahead and try."

As soon as the castle door was slammed in Finn's and Sir Jacobus's faces, the skies opened up and it started pouring. It was a good thing, too, because the food fight the previous evening had spilled out onto the lawn and there was still maple syrup and tufts of cotton candy everywhere.

"They're bluffing," Sir Jacobus said confidently as the water pounded down on them in great torrential sheets.

"Are you sure?" Finn asked. It had seemed like Lord and Lady Gooddog were quite serious. He and Sir Jacobus hadn't even been allowed to pack their things. They'd just been shoved out the door.

"You just watch," Sir Jacobus assured him. "Any

minute now they are going to start worrying that I'll catch a cold or something while I'm standing out here in this mess. They'll get all nervous and fling open the doors any minute, begging me to come back."

"If you say so, dude," Finn said, loyally standing at his side.

Five hours later, and the rain was still coming down in buckets. "I don't think they're opening the doors back up," Finn finally said. "I mean, if they were worried about you catching a cold, I'm sure they would have said something by now."

"I can't believe they're doing this," Sir Jacobus said, sadly shaking his head.

"Look at the bright side," his Hu-manservant told him. "Now you don't have to save Lady Rainicorn from that witch or get married or anything. You can just keep being an untamed scoundrel."

"No way," Sir Jacobus said, a fierce determination

gleaming in his eyes. "I'm going to save Lady Rainicorn from that horrible witch and then I'm going to woo her."

"Woo?" Finn asked, a bit surprised.

"Woo," Sir Jacobus insisted.

"Wow, man, I've never seen you this passionate about a girl," Finn said. "Not ever. And I've seen you flirt with a lot of girls."

"That's because the girls I was flirting with were never Lady Rainicorn. We're soul mates. We are meant to be together."

"And you got all that from almost asking her to dance?" Finn had to wonder.

"That's right," Sir Jacobus insisted.

"Huh." Finn thought it over. "So, where do we go from here?"

Sir Jacobus turned and started walking toward the village. "Well, there's where I go, and there's where you go," he said.

"What does that mean?"

"I'm going to the Licorice Lion Inn to get warm and dry," Sir Jacobus explained. "And you're going to go find out where that nasty witch is keeping Lady Rainicorn prisoner."

Finn frowned. "That doesn't sound fair."

"No." Sir Jacobus had to agree, patting his servant on the shoulder. "It really doesn't."

It was growing dark by the time Finn finally arrived at the Licorice Lion Inn. He was exhausted, wet, and chilled to the bone. "Hot apple cider," he requested from the barkeep as he slumped in a chair by the fire.

"So?" Sir Jacobus asked, without so much as a friendly greeting. "Did you find out where that witch is keeping Lady Rainicorn?"

"I'm fine, Sir Jacobus. Thanks for asking. How was your day after you left me to slog around in the mud while you came to sit here in this toasty inn?" Finn wasn't in the best of moods.

"It was okay," his master told him. "To be honest with you, the sandwiches here are a little disappointing. I only ate six before I just gave up."

"Do you even understand sarcasm?" Finn asked as the barkeep set his steaming mug of apple cider down in front of him.

"Not anymore," Sir Jacobus informed him. "I'm too in love with Lady Rainicorn to recognize the emotions of other people."

Finn gave him a flat look. "You are being so lame, dude. I'm telling you now: You're being lame."

"Was that sarcasm, too?" Sir Jacobus signaled to the barkeep that he would like another apple cider for himself.

"No." Finn shook his head. "Not even close."

"So tell me what you found out about the love of my life," Sir Jacobus prompted. "I've been sitting here for hours. It felt like it took you forever."

Taking a big swig of his cider, Finn answered. "Well, it turns out the witch is holding Lady Rainicorn prisoner in an island fortress surrounded by treacherous waters."

Sir Jacobus frowned. "How treacherous?"

"There're supposed to be these horrible sea monsters that live in the water surrounding the castle," Finn told him. "They attack any boat that tries to weigh anchor there."

"I knew it," Sir Jacobus said, slamming down his fist and causing the cider in Finn's mug to slosh onto the table. "I bet you the witch has cast an evil spell on some poor innocent giant squid or something to attack any boat that gets even close. She sounds like a real jerk."

"Well, there's nothing we can do about that," Finn said with a sigh. "I mean, we can't fight a giant sea monster. Guess now we should just focus on finding a way to make a living. What do you think about turning outlaw?"

"I can't think about any career choice until I know my lady is safe," was the untamed scoundrel's reply.

Finn sighed. "Do we have to?"

"Either you're with me or we part ways here," Sir Jacobus told him.

"Well . . . ," Finn said, mulling it over. "Let's stick together," he finally said. "I'll help you rescue Lady Rainicorn. I am, after all, your best friend and humble servant."

"Okay, great," Sir Jacobus said. He knew he could count on his good buddy and Hu-manservant to be loyal no matter what. "Tomorrow morning we'll get a boat, deal with the sea-monster thingy, and then take down the witch. I should be wooing Lady Rainicorn by lunch."

"Sounds good," Finn agreed. "But how are we going to get a boat?"

Sir Jacobus shrugged. "I'm the son of Lord and Lady Gooddog. I'm sure a ton of people would be happy to lend us one."

CHAPTER 6

"Absolutely not," the ship's captain said, setting his chin. "By my family's tartan, I wouldn't lend the son of Lord and Lady Gooddog a toothpick, much less my ship. I depend on that vessel for my livelihood. Let that spoiled brat go bother his parents for a loan if he wants to go out pleasure cruising."

"But that's what I'm trying to tell you," Sir Jacobus said. "I'm Jacobus Gooddog and I'm not going out pleasure cruising. I just need to borrow your boat so I can sail into some treacherous waters, fight a witch, and save my true love. It shouldn't take more than half a day, tops."

"Well, since you put it that way," the captain said, "no, no, and no. I really can't say no enough."

Sir Jacobus hung his head as he walked back up the dock to where Finn was waiting for him on the pier. "I'm not having much luck getting us a boat," he confessed.

"How many captains have you asked?" his servant asked.

"About fourteen, I think."

"Oh." Finn nodded, his face solemn. "Did you happen to mention to any of them that you are the son of Lord and Lady Gooddog?"

"Yeah, but that seemed to make them all more convinced that they should say no." Sir Jacobus threw up his paws in disgust.

"Maybe you should try telling them that you're *not* the son of Lord and Lady Gooddog. That might help," Finn suggested.

"I think it's too late for that now," Sir Jacobus grumbled.

"Hmmm . . ." Finn nodded some more, chewing the side of his lip, deep in thought. "I think we might have to borrow one."

"That's what I've been trying to tell you," Sir Jacobus said, sounding a little exasperated. "I've asked more than a dozen captains, and all were unwilling to lend us a boat. Haven't you been listening?"

"Yeah, well, maybe we have to borrow a boat and just not ask anybody before we take it," Finn suggested.

The son of Lord and Lady Gooddog was a bit shocked. "Isn't that stealing?"

Finn shrugged. "You say tomato. I say potato."

"What are you talking about?"

"It's an expression," the Hu-manservant insisted.

Making a face, Sir Jacobus asked, "Are you sure that's a real expression?"

"I don't know," Finn said with a shrug, "I'm not in charge of making that stuff up. But I do know there's a pretty nice boat at the end of the dock that we could borrow for the morning if we do it quick before the owners come back."

When Finn said "a boat," what he really meant was a ship, a real beauty with a tall mast and a new, white sail all ready to be unfurled. After a few minutes of vigorous work, Finn and Sir Jacobus were out on the water and headed for the witch's island fortress.

"This is going to be totally rad," Sir Jacobus said, rubbing his paws together once they were well underway. "I can't wait to start wooing Lady Rainicorn. I've never felt this way about anyone before."

"That's totally bumps," Finn told him, "but don't get distracted with your plans to be all lovey-dovey before we get there. Right now we should be keeping our eyes open for the sea monster." He eyed the blue water suspiciously. The stories he'd heard while he was out gathering information had left him very nervous.

"What's it look like?" his master wanted to know.

"How the heck should I know?" was Finn's reply. "If it's big and mean and coming out of the sea, then that's probably it."

Sir Jacobus found a spyglass in the captain's cabin and started scanning the horizon. "I think I see the island," he said. "There's a big castle with two towers on it." He lowered the instrument and looked fiercely toward the island. "I bet you my lady is locked in one of those—ouch!"

"What?" Finn was confused. He'd been steering the ship and not really paying attention to what his friend was saying. "Are you all right?"

"Something just bit me on the ear," Sir Jacobus told him. His left ear was glowing red and a bit swollen.

Finn frowned. "What bit you, man?" He scanned the sky. "Like a bug or a bird or . . . *yeowch*! What the glob was that?" he asked, looking at a bright red mark on his arm.

"It came out of the water," Sir Jacobus told him. It had happened very quickly, but he had witnessed the attack. "It looked like some kind of little fish or something."

"Little? Like how little?" Finn asked. The pain in his arm didn't feel so little. "Hey, look out!" He swatted at the air above Gooddog's head, knocking a small fish onto the deck.

"What is it?" Sir Jacobus asked, squinting down as the little creature flopped around, its jaw snapping. "It looks like a sardine."

"It looks like a rabid sardine," Finn corrected him. "Why would that thing be jumping out of the water and trying to—ouch! Ouch! *Yeowch!*" Dozens of the tiny fish started flinging themselves out of the water and onto the deck in an attempt to bite Finn and Sir Jacobus.

"Make the ship go faster!" Sir Jacobus yelled as he swatted at the hundreds of sardines that were piling onto the deck. At least a dozen of the fish were biting at his arms and legs.

"I can't!" was Finn's reply. He was steering with one hand and swatting at sardines with the other. "We can only go as fast as the wind says we can."

"We need to get some extra wind," Sir Jacobus cried, the sardines leaving red welts wherever they managed to bite. Leaping into the air, Sir Jacobus grabbed the mast and flattened out his body into a big sheet, trying to make himself into an extra sail. "Ouch! Ouch! Ouch! Ouch! Ouch! Why isn't this working?"

"Try being a net instead," Finn told him. "I'll look for a weapon or something belowdecks."

Sir Jacobus stopped trying to be a sail and turned his right paw into a giant net. He scooped at the sardines that were piling up on the deck and flung them overboard. "Ouch, ouch, ouch," he wailed each time he scooped up a new load of the angry little fish. They refused to stop biting him. "Hurry up, Finn!" He wondered if his Hu-manservant was just hiding in the captain's quarters or something.

There was a loud clanging that sounded like Finn had tripped over a pile of pans. Dozens of the little fish quickly flopped for the edge of the ship and flung themselves overboard. "What was that?" Sir Jacobus called.

"What?" Finn's voice could be heard from belowdecks. He sounded irritated, but he was the one belowdecks, so Sir Jacobus didn't think he had the right.

"What was that loud noise you just made?" Sir Jacobus shouted back.

"I tripped over a large sack of empty cans," was the reply. "There are a ton of empty cans down here."

"Well, do it again," Sir Jacobus told him. "I don't think the fish like that noise."

"Like this?" Finn clanged the cans again and more fish scampered off the deck of the ship.

"Louder! Louder!" Sir Jacobus shouted. "Keep doing it. They hate that noise."

Finn staggered onto the deck slamming around a burlap sack full of cans. Dozens of the crazed sardines dove for the sea. "What the zip? What are those funky-junk fish afraid of?"

"Who cares?" his master exclaimed. "Just keep banging."

Each time Finn rattled the cans, more of the sardines fled the ship. Finally, there were only a few left that Sir Jacobus was able to kick over the side.

"That was really weird," Finn said, once they were sardine-free. "What do you think it is about empty cans that sardines don't like?"

"I have no idea," Sir Jacobus said with a shrug. "But let's not lose that bag of cans for the trip back." He turned, squinting courageously toward the horizon to see where they were and exclaimed, "Hey, look! We're almost at the island."

CHAPTER 7

Minutes later Finn and Sir Jacobus weighed anchor and were climbing over the rocks that ringed the shoreline of the small island. "Okay," Finn said, happy to have both of his feet back on solid ground. "Let's get this over with. I'm getting hungry."

"Look," Sir Jacobus said, pointing at the massive castle fortress. "I can see the witch looking out the window at the top of that tower." Marceline waved at them, but it didn't look like a friendly wave. "I guess she sees us," Sir Jacobus said in a whisper.

"Dude, isn't that Lady Rainicorn looking out the window of the other tower?" Finn asked.

It was indeed Lady Rainicorn. She looked gorgeous, even at a distance. Her mane was blowing in a light breeze, and the sun was shining off her rainbow skin, even though it was cloudy everywhere else.

"You're right," Sir Jacobus said with a gasp, small hearts taking the place of the pupils in his eyes. "She's just as beautiful as I remembered."

"If you say so, dude," Finn told him.

"I'm coming, my lady!" the untamed scoundrel shouted. She didn't look in their direction, so perhaps she hadn't noticed them. A few moments later she disappeared from sight. "She might be in trouble," Sir Jacobus said. He started running over the rocks and small shrubs that filled the landscape. "I'm here to save—*yeowch*!"

"What happened? More sardines?" Finn asked, flinching and swatting wildly at the air. He'd left the sack of empty cans on the ship and was feeling a bit panicked.

"No. A splinter," Sir Jacobus said with a yelp. "From one of these stupid shrubs."

"A splinter?" Finn wasn't sure he'd heard his friend correctly.

"Yeah. But, like, a really, really painful splinter." He tried pulling the thing out with his teeth.

"I hate those," Finn had to admit. It started to rain a little. He wished he'd been wearing a jacket when he was thrown out of the Gooddogs' castle. "Maybe they have tweezers on the ship," he suggested, thinking it would also be nice to get out of the rain.

"No, I can get it," Sir Jacobus insisted, gnawing some more at his paw. It started raining harder.

"Man, I am really hungry," Finn said, shivering a little. He looked up and saw that the beautiful witch was still watching them from her window in the tower. She was frowning. The rain started coming down in buckets. "Let's go back to the ship, find tweezers, and get something to eat while we wait for this rain to stop," he suggested, not feeling supercomfortable with the witch watching their every move.

"Good idea," Sir Jacobus said, his words muffled by his paw in his mouth.

"Man, I cannot wait to dig into some chow," Finn said, once they were back on the ship and heading belowdecks. "I saw a ton of canned goods in the cupboard so I bet there's a bunch of tasty stuff to eat."

"Oh good," Sir Jacobus said, finally dislodging the sliver from his paw. "I feel like spaghetti."

Finn opened the cupboard. "You're in luck," he told his friend. "There's tomato sauce." He reached for the can. "What the flip? It's empty," he exclaimed, throwing down the can. "Why would somebody keep an empty can in a cupboard?"

"Beats me," Sir Jacobus said with a shrug. "I guess I could eat stew, instead." He went to grab a large can of stew and was surprised how light it was.

"Hey, wait a minute. This can is empty, too."

"Oh no!" Finn felt a wave of dread wash over him. He flung the cupboard doors all the way open and started pulling out can after can. "Empty, empty, they're all empty!" he wailed.

"Who would do such a thing?" Sir Jacobus said, completely bewildered as his stomach started to seriously growl.

"I know," Finn said, slamming the cupboard doors shut. "It was that witch."

"What do you mean?" Sir Jacobus wanted to know. It seemed unlikely the witch had been able to sneak aboard the ship and empty all the cans without them noticing.

"I mean, think about it," Finn said. "First, no one would lend you a boat, so we had to special-borrow one. Then we got attacked by rabid sardines. Then you got that superpainful splinter and it started raining megahard. Now we're stuck on a boat that doesn't even have any food." Finn thumped a timber with his fist. "That witch has obviously set up some kind of curse or something so that we can't get to the island. This is all some kind of plot to prevent you from wooing Lady Rainicorn."

"I knew it!" Sir Jacobus thundered. "We have got to go fight that witch and save my lady."

"We can't just run in there and fight her. She's too powerful," the Hu-manservant insisted. "She's all magical and stuff."

"But what can we do?" Sir Jacobus wailed. "The witch has got my beautiful lady held prisoner."

"We need to get some magic for ourselves."

"I guess we could go back to the mainland and find a powerful warlock or sorcerer or something," Sir Jacobus concluded. "We'll need to find one that knows how to battle a superbad witch."

"Don't sweat it," Finn assured his boss. "I know just the guy."

The untamed scoundrel and his faithful servant stalwartly headed back whence they came, pounding on empty cans the whole way for fear of another sardine attack. They anchored their ship just where they'd found it and no one seemed to be the wiser. "Now, where's this magic man of yours?" Sir Jacobus said as they strolled into town.

"Here we are," Finn said, stopping in front of a store called The Little Green Butcher Shop.

"Would you stop thinking about your stomach for once?" said Sir Jacobus, who was feeling irritable, probably from lack of food. There was, after all, a huge display of all kinds of meats in the window.

"But this is it," Finn insisted. "This guy's supposed to be a sorcerer and a butcher."

"If you say so." Sir Jacobus shrugged. A small bell chimed as they entered the shop.

"Can I help you, *gentlemen*?" a voice sang out, emphasizing the word *gentlemen* in a weird way. A very tall man stepped out from behind a counter that was displaying meats of every variety. The man had very long arms and legs and a long body to match.

"Um yeah," Finn told him. "We're looking for something very special and I heard you were the man to see."

"What do you *need*? Pork shoulder? *Hummingbird* tongue? We have it *here*. Frozen mammoth? Chihuahua *flank*? It's not a *problem*." The man singsonged his way through the meats he had to offer.

"Actually," Finn said in a hushed voice, "we're looking for something along the lines of a witch."

The store clerk straightened to his full height. "We do not sell witch here," he said, sounding indignant and not singing a single word.

"No, we're not looking for anything from the butcher. We want to use your other services." Finn gave the man a very broad wink and a significant nod.

"You see, there's this witch in this castle," Sir

Jacobus interjected. "And she's holding my true love prisoner. We want to save her, but the witch has cast a powerful spell that is making it superhard to storm the castle."

"Tell me what *happened* when you went to the *castle*," the tall man singsonged.

"Well, first of all, no one would lend us a boat. And I'm the son of Lord and Lady Gooddog," Sir Jacobus told him. "Then we got attacked by rabid sardines when we were sailing to the island that has the castle. Then I got a splinter, and then it started raining, and then there was no food on the boat that we had to secretly borrow."

"What a *nightmare*," the man said, projecting empathy. "I can't *believe* you managed to survive at *all*."

"Yeah, so that's when we decided we needed some help," Finn told the butcher. "Real help. Your kind of help."

"I understand you *completely*," the tall man said. "I have a *wonderful* haggis that is just what you're looking *for*."

"What's a haggis?" Finn wanted to know.

"How can you live in the Kingdom of *Plaid* and not know about *haggis*?" the man sang out, seriously surprised.

"I don't know." Finn shrugged. "No one's ever brought it up so far."

"Haggis is a specialty of Plaid," Sir Jacobus told him. "It's like wearing a kilt or having a family tartan."

"Fine by me, but what is it?" the Hu-manservant asked. "I'm pretty darn sure I've never seen one in the castle."

"Yeah . . . ," Sir Jacobus said evasively. "That's because they're . . . um . . . you know. Kind of gross."

"Gross how?" Finn asked, still not understanding.

"Well, you start with a sheep's stomach," Sir Jacobus began. "And then you dice up a bunch of other sheep organs and you put them inside."

"You're kidding?" Finn asked, the mere thought making him a little green. He wondered if that was how the butcher shop got its name.

"No, he is not *kidding*," the magical man intervened. "But you also add *oatmeal* and *spices* to make an organ-meat stuffing and cook it real *good*."

"Yeah, but then what do you do with it after it's cooked?" Finn wanted to know.

"You're *supposed* to eat *it*," the butcher told him.

"What?" Finn was confused. "Cooked stomach with organ-meat stuffing. Do you mean on a dare or something?"

"No," the butcher insisted. "For *dinner*."

"You have to be flippin' kidding me." Finn just couldn't wrap his head around it. "Why would anybody in their right mind want to eat that?" he asked. "It makes no sense."

"Maybe it'll make more *sense* if I tell you in

this *song*," the tall, thin man crooned. He was obviously about to launch into a very informative musical number.

"Wait a minute. Wait a minute," Sir Jacobus interrupted. "We don't have time to stand around while you sing some crazy song," he said. "I need to save Lady Rainicorn from the witch, so do you have something magic we can use to free her from the castle or don't you?"

"That's what I've been trying to *tell you*," the magical butcher said. "I can enchant this piece of *haggis*," he said, holding up a large serving of the unappetizing meat. "I can do it right *now* and it will help you breach the *castle* and save your *lady* love."

"So, what are we waiting for?" Sir Jacobus asked. "Enchant that disgusting organ meat."

"It's just that I feel obligated to *warn you*," the magic man sang. "Once I enchant the meat and you say the words that cause it to *come to life*, then it will not *stop* until your enemy is *vanquished*."

"Sounds good," Sir Jacobus told him, rubbing his paws together at the thought of getting one over on the evil witch. "You have my permission to do your stuff."

"As you *wish*," the magical butcher said. He placed the haggis on a butcher's block, closed his eyes, and waved his hands over the meat. "Trick or *treat*, smell my *feet*, give me something *good* to *eat*." The sorcerer's hands started glowing a bright blue. He continued with, "*Duplicate*, *conjugate*, keep on going, don't *debate*." The haggis took on the unearthly blue glow. "Once you *begin*, you will not *rest* until you have done your *best*. *To win!*" he bellowed. There was a bright flash of blue light and then everything returned to normal.

"You kind of lost the whole rhyme scheme at the end there, didn't you?" Sir Jacobus commented, wondering if that would be a problem.

"It worked *beautifully*," the magic man insisted.

"All you have to do is say the words 'Haggis is better than kidney *pie*' and you should have *no* trouble beating that nasty old *witch*."

Sir Jacobus made a face. "Haggis is better than . . . ?"

"*Don't* say it *now!*" the sorcerer bellowed, snatching up the haggis and quickly wrapping it in brown paper. "That would be a *disaster*. You can only say it when battling your *enemy*. And then you should only use it if absolutely *necessary*. This magic is very *powerful*."

"Got it," Finn said. "How much do we owe you?"

"Just make sure I'm invited to the *wedding* and I'll consider your debt *paid*," the singing butcher said.

"It's a deal," Sir Jacobus told him. "If there's a wedding, we'll make sure to invite you."

On the way out of the shop, Finn had to laugh. "Wedding? We sure got one over on him. I guess that guy didn't know your reputation as an untamed scoundrel."

CHAPTER 8

By the time Finn and Sir Jacobus got back to the docks, the boat they had originally "borrowed" had a bunch of surly-looking men standing around on it. "Why don't we look to borrow someone else's boat?" Finn suggested in a clenched whisper.

"Good idea," Sir Jacobus agreed and they quickly veered off in a new direction.

Finding an unattended boat wasn't as easy the second time. Apparently, word had spread quickly that someone was borrowing vessels without permission. They grabbed sandwiches and slices of apple pie to keep their strength up, but it still took them over an hour to find a new craft to borrow without anyone noticing.

"What do you think would happen if we got caught borrowing this boat?" Sir Jacobus asked as they sneaked aboard the unattended schooner.

"I think we'd be thrown in jail," Finn said, not bothering to mince his words. "The law doesn't look kindly on people who borrow boats without asking."

Once they got away from the dock for a while, it was smooth sailing. The sky was clear, and Sir Jacobus was at his leisure to think about wooing his lady love. But as they drew closer to the sardine-infested waters, both he and his servant grew more tense.

"Maybe I'd better go belowdecks and get some empty cans," Finn suggested. "Just so we're ready."

"Good idea," Sir Jacobus agreed. His ear was still throbbing from the first attack.

Finn scooted down the stairs, scanning the galley for a sack of cans. "Where can they be?" he wondered aloud as he searched. "They've got to be around here somewhere."

"Finn," Sir Jacobus called down. "Hurry it up. We're getting pretty close to sardine time."

"I'm looking," he shouted back. And he was looking, increasingly frantically. "Where would I keep a bag of empty cans if I owned a ship?" he asked himself.

"Finn!" the untamed scoundrel bellowed. "You really need to chop chop. The water's starting to bubble."

And it was true. There were thousands of tiny little bubbles rising to the surface of the water and popping. Sir Jacobus had the horrible feeling that each bubble represented a rabid sardine just waiting to breach the surface of the ocean to try to take a bite out of his hide. "Finn!" he called belowdecks again, sounding on the verge of panic.

"Cans. Cans. Where are the stupid cans?" Finn

pulled open closets and rifled through drawers. Finally, out of desperation, he flung open the cupboard. "Here they are!" he exclaimed with relief. "Why do people keep empty cans in the cupboard?"

But the cans weren't empty. They were the exact opposite of empty. "Full?" Finn had to wonder as he yanked out a can of baked beans. "Full," he said again as he grabbed a can of stewed tomatoes. "Full, full, full. These cans are all full."

"Fiiiinnn," came a wail from above. "*Yeowch!* Ouch! Ouch! Sardines!!!"

"Why is there food in these cans?" Finn demanded. Every can in the cupboard actually had something in it. "I need a can opener. Right now!"

Finn yanked open the galley's silverware drawer, but he pulled too hard, and the contents of the drawer spilled out, crashing onto the floor. "Where's the opener?" he wanted to know as he scrambled through the utensils.

"Ouch! *Yeowch! Yipe!*" Sir Jacobus cried as he tried desperately to fight off the sardines while still steering the schooner. "Hurry up, Finn!" he bellowed. "Now's not the time to be making yourself a snack."

Finn came charging up the stairs, his arms full of cans. He tripped and the cans went tumbling across the deck. "I can't find an opener," he insisted. "All the stupid cans are full." The sardines immediately started biting him. "Ouch! Flippin' sardines!"

Holding onto the ship's wheel with one paw, Sir Jacobus reached with the other paw for the head of an ax. "I've got it," he said and with a *thwack!* he split one of the cans in half. Spaghetti sprayed everywhere.

Finn scrambled after the two halves of the can, shook out the remaining spaghetti, and started pounding them together, making a small clanging noise. A few sardines flopped over the side of the ship. "Cut more cans," he shouted.

Sir Jacobus started hacking through cans while

Finn emptied the split ones and kept on banging. He found an empty burlap sack and tossed the cans in there so it was easier to cause a commotion. At first only a few dozen sardines fled the ship, but as the noise grew louder, more sardines decided to give up the assault and leap back into the ocean.

By the time the last sardine had given up and retreated to the water, the deck of the ship was covered in split pea soup, creamed corn, and beef stew. "I was going to say we should have a snack to fortify ourselves for fighting the witch," Sir Jacobus said, "but I've completely lost my appetite."

"Huh?" Finn looked up from where he was snacking on a mound of spilled spaghetti.

"Never mind," his master told him. "We're almost there."

After they weighed anchor, Sir Jacobus insisted that they wash down the ship before they rescued

Lady Rainicorn. "But why?" Finn wanted to know. "We're rescuing her. Isn't that enough?"

"I'm not taking my true love back to the mainland in a ship that's covered in digestible edibles," Sir Jacobus explained, standing firm with a mop in paw. "That's totally not romantic."

As they scrubbed, Finn kept glancing toward the castle. "Look," he said. "The witch is totally watching us."

"Let her watch," Sir Jacobus said with toss of his head. "We've got the haggis."

"Yeah, so, what do you think the haggis will do once you say the magic words?" Finn wanted to know.

"I don't know," the Gooddog said with a shrug. "But I bet it's going to be totally algebraic."

"We should listen to the magic man's advice, though, don't you think?" Finn urged. "I mean, maybe we can save Lady Rainicorn without using the haggis."

"Yeah," his boss agreed. "We'll give that old witch a chance to be reasonable, but if she refuses, then it's haggis time."

CHAPTER 9

"Okay," Finn said, once everything was shipshape on the ship. "Let's get this whole saving-the-damsel-in-distress thing over with. How do you want to take that witch down?"

Sir Jacobus scratched his head. "Maybe you can catapult me into the tower window and I can just fight her from there?"

"All right." Finn rather liked the idea of catapulting his boss. "But I didn't see a catapult on the ship."

"Was there a cannon?" Sir Jacobus wanted to know. "You could shoot me out of a cannon."

"I don't think so, dude. But that would have been cool."

"Okay, well, I'll just hang on to two trees. You stretch my body back really far, aim me at the tower window, and then let go," Sir Jacobus said.

"That's not fair," the Hu-manservant said, stamping his foot. "I want to fight the witch, too. Why should you have all the fun?"

"I'll open the door for you or something once I'm inside," his master assured him.

Finn was reluctant to be left behind, but finally said, "All right. Just don't forget about me. And don't fight the witch all by yourself. In fact, just leave the battle to me. I'll need something to do while you're wooing Lady Rainicorn."

They found two sturdy trees in front of the castle. Sir Jacobus wrapped a paw tightly around each. "Okay, you can stretch me now."

Finn grabbed his master around the waist and

started pulling, causing Sir Jacobus's arms to stretch longer and longer. "Tell me when," he said.

"A bit more," Sir Jacobus told him. His arms were getting really long and it was hard to hold on. "Okay, now aim me toward the window and let go."

Doing his best to line his master up so he would fly right through the tower's open window, Finn said, "Okay, on three. One. Two. Three." He let go.

Sir Jacobus's arms snapped back like when a stretched rubber band is released. He let go of the trees and an instant later was flying through the air directly at the castle tower.

Unfortunately for Sir Jacobus Gooddog, he wasn't flying directly at the castle tower's window. He hit the hard stone of the tower just below the window with a loud *splat*.

"Are you all right?" Finn asked, holding back his amusement until he knew for sure that his buddy wasn't hurt.

"I don't think so," Sir Jacobus said with a groan. "Actually, I'm stuck."

That's when Marceline the witch appeared at the tower window. She had a broom with her and used it to scrape Sir Jacobus off the side of the tower. "Why are you holding Lady Rainicorn prisoner?" Sir Jacobus demanded as he tumbled to the ground.

"Huh?" the witch asked, but it was too late. The Gooddog was already falling and she couldn't hear his question clearly. "You're welcome," she shouted anyway, just assuming Sir Jacobus was making some sort of attempt at good manners.

"That was flippin' hilarious," Finn exclaimed once his master was on his feet and didn't appear hurt. "Let's do it again."

"Nah," Sir Jacobus said, waving him off with an unsteady paw. "I think we'd better think of something else."

"Like what?" Finn asked. "I'm pretty sure I could

slingshot you into the window if we tried it again."
The Gooddog didn't look convinced, so he added,
"Come on. One more try."

"All right," Sir Jacobus said, a bit reluctantly.
"But aim higher this time."

On the second try, Finn aimed a little too high,
and his lord went sailing over the top of the castle
tower. Fortunately, instead of crashing to the ground,
Sir Jacobus landed in the water on the far side of the
island. It was, after all, a very small island.

"Third time's a charm," Finn insisted once Sir
Jacobus had hauled himself out of the ocean and
walked back to the castle. "I promise I won't miss
this time. I swear."

And he didn't miss. Sir Jacobus was propelled
directly at the tower window. Unfortunately, the
witch had closed the shutters, and so Sir Jacobus
found himself tasting wood rather than tasting
sweet victory.

"Okay, I've got it figured out," Finn said, once his master had peeled himself off the side of the tower. "This time we'll . . ."

"You are totally poo-brained if you think I'm doing that again," Sir Jacobus said, cutting him off.

"Well then how are you going to get the witch down?" Finn asked. "It's not like we can bust down the door or anything. I mean, it's a fortress."

"I'm sick of all this messing around." Sir Jacobus thumped his fist against his other paw as he shouted, "Release the haggis!"

CHAPTER 10

"The haggis?" Finn asked in surprise. "What the glob? I thought that magic dude said not to use the haggis unless we really, really needed it."

"We do really, really need it," Sir Jacobus insisted stubbornly. "I don't have all day to keep slamming into that tower. We've got to save Lady Rainicorn so I can start wooing her. Let's just get this witch out of the way so I can get to the good stuff."

"If you say so." Finn shrugged. "But are you sure you want to start a battle that won't end until the witch is vanquished?"

Sir Jacobus gingerly touched his nose, which was

still sore from when he slammed into the shutters that the witch had closed. "Yeah, I'm sure."

"Fine by me," Finn said, unwrapping the brown paper from the haggis. "I guess you'd better say the magic words."

Clearing his throat, Sir Jacobus said, "Haggis is better than kidney pie."

The haggis just sat there, looking like a disgusting piece of haggis.

"Try again," Finn told him.

"Haggis is better than kidney pie," the untamed scoundrel repeated, a bit louder this time. There was a faint blue glow about the haggis, but it disappeared after only a few seconds. "Awww, man," Sir Jacobus grumbled. "This haggis is a dud."

Finn poked at it, frowning. "Maybe you're not doing it right."

"Am too," Sir Jacobus insisted. "I'm saying the exact words that magical butcher said."

"Yeah, but are you saying them the exact way he said them?" Finn asked. "You should try it like that."

"But I'd feel like a total ding-dong," Sir Jacobus insisted.

"Do you want a magical haggis or not?" Finn asked him. "'Cause otherwise we have to go back to smacking you into the tower."

"Okay, fine," Sir Jacobus said, rolling his eyes. "Haggis is better than kidney *pie*," he sang, waving his arms around for good measure.

The haggis immediately took on an intense blue glow. "It's working," Finn whispered excitedly. And then he added, "Holy glob!" as the haggis stood up and started hopping around. "It's really working."

"Hey, wait a minute," Sir Jacobus said, staring after the enchanted meat. "Didn't we just have one haggis? Now I see two."

It was true. The haggis had duplicated itself as it hopped around in front of the castle. Another moment after that and there were four enchanted sheep stomachs filled with minced organs, plus spices, of course, bouncing around like bunnies. "Man is that gross," Finn couldn't help but remark. "That witch isn't going to know what hit her."

Each haggis doubled itself again and then again. They started marching like a battalion of soldiers in straight lines, bouncing their way closer and closer to the castle.

"How many of them are there now?" Sir Jacobus asked after a few minutes, still completely amazed.

"At least a hundred," Finn told him. "And there's more every minute."

The entire lawn in front of the castle was filled with enchanted haggis, in perfectly straight lines. They stopped marching and stood still, as if at attention.

"What are they waiting for?" Sir Jacobus asked, in a half whisper. An entire army of enchanted sheep stomachs was pretty intimidating.

"I think they're waiting for your orders," was Finn's reply. "What do you want them to do?"

"Oh." Sir Jacobus Gooddog scratched his chin in thought. "I kind of thought they'd already know what to do."

His servant shrugged. "Obviously not." After several moments of nothing happening but a new haggis joining the army every few seconds, Finn cleared his throat. "Uh . . . I think you'd better tell them what to do before we're knee-deep in these things."

"Um, yeah . . . I get that," Sir Jacobus said. "I was just standing here wondering if maybe this was actually a really bad idea."

Finn had to laugh. "Like that's ever stopped us before."

"You're right," Sir Jacobus said with a decisive nod. He stepped forward and raised his voice.

"Attention all haggises . . . or haggi . . . or however you like to be addressed." The haggis seemed to be listening. "Okay, um, like, the lady I love is being held prisoner in that castle." He gestured toward the castle, even though it was the only building on the island. "And she's guarded by an evil witch—"

"Actually, the witch doesn't look that dangerous," Finn interrupted, "but you've got to trust us when we say she's evil."

Sir Jacobus shot his servant an annoyed look. "Okay, well . . . anyway," he addressed the haggis again. "We need to get into the tower so we can stop the witch and free my lady love. Anything you can do to help us would be really cool."

Finn scrunched his nose. "Um . . . are you sure that's specific enough?" he asked. "I mean, you left things pretty open for the haggis to do whatever they want."

"I don't think they have the power to do what

they want. I think they just have to do what I want," Sir Jacobus said. Still, he shot a nervous look in the direction of the organ-stuffed stomachs. "Wait a minute. What are they doing?" he exclaimed.

The haggis army was marching toward the castle, but they weren't headed toward the tower that held the witch. The haggis were headed toward the tower where Lady Rainicorn was imprisoned. The shutters were shut, but Sir Jacobus knew his lady was in there, probably in shackles without a lot of nice things to eat.

"Wait a minute! Wait a minute!" Sir Jacobus sprinted to get in front of the stomach meat. "You're about to swarm the wrong tower." He pointed toward the tower window where Marceline was watching their every move. She had opened her shutters again. "That's the witch's tower over there," he instructed them. "Attack!"

CHAPTER 11

In unison the haggis turned and marched toward the correct tower. Marceline was not looking comfortable from her bird's-eye view. "We've got her now," Finn said, cackling with glee.

The battalion of sheep stomachs stopped in front of the witch's tower. They stood in their straight lines as if waiting for orders. One haggis hopped around in front of the rest like a general reviewing his troops.

A group of the stomach meat turned and approached Sir Jacobus. "Uh . . . ," he said, taking a few nervous steps backward. "What do you think they want?"

"Beats me," said Finn, who also found his feet shuffling away from the strange enchanted meat.

The haggis pounced on Sir Jacobus and grabbed his right arm. They began pulling on it to stretch it longer and longer. "Hey, hey, hey now . . . what are you doing?" the untamed scoundrel asked. He wasn't used to having his arms stretch without giving permission.

Once the haggis thought Sir Jacobus's arm was a sizeable length, they began using him like a living slingshot to fire haggis after haggis at the witch's tower window. They had much better aim than Finn. Almost every shot would have been a direct hit, except for the fact that Marceline had somehow pulled out her ax guitar and was swatting the haggis back at them whenever one got close enough for her to reach.

More haggis grabbed Sir Jacobus's left arm and began stretching it. "I somehow thought the haggis were supposed to get into the castle without my help," the Gooddog moaned.

"Think again," his servant told him. "The haggis are just using whatever they can find to get the job done." Just then a few haggis pushed him over and yanked off one of his shoes.

"Hey!" Finn shouted. "I'm using that." But the stomach meat ignored him, firing the shoe at the tower using one of Sir Jacobus's slingshot arms. Marceline easily deflected the shoe with her ax guitar, and Finn scurried to retrieve it.

"I don't see how firing shoes at the tower is actually going to bring the witch down," Sir Jacobus grumbled. "This isn't working. Try something else," he shouted at the haggis.

The haggis in charge must have given a new order because the stomach meat released Sir Jacobus's arms. They started hopping one on top of the other, stacking themselves taller and taller until they formed great haggis chains tottering toward the open window of the witch's tower.

At first Marceline was using her ax guitar to knock off the haggis on the top of the teetering chains. But those were quickly replaced by new stomachs intent on entering her window. So the witch began waiting until the pillars of haggis got very close, then she would snatch one off the top and throw it at the bottom haggis. If her aim was true, the whole line of stomach meat would collapse and have to start all over again.

Marceline had a good arm. She was able to knock down the pillars of haggis pretty quickly. It soon became obvious to everyone, including the stomach meat, that this was not the way they were going to gain entrance to the fortress.

A few of the haggis started hopping around at Sir Jacobus's feet, bumping into his legs. "Gross. What do they want?" he asked, not too thrilled about being nudged by sheep intestine.

"I think they're looking for you to tell them

what to do next," Finn said, doing his best to keep a safe distance from the stomachs. "I think they're out of ideas."

"How the zip am I supposed to know what they should do?" He turned to the haggis. "Fly into the window and subdue the witch," he commanded. None of the stomachs moved, but they did appear to be looking at him questioningly, if that was possible for something without a face.

"How about a giant pyramid?" Finn suggested.

Sir Jacobus gave his servant a curious look. "Why would I want to sit in a giant pyramid made out of sheep stomachs?" The haggis began to twitch a little, as if forming a giant pyramid over Sir Jacobus was something they were willing to consider.

"I didn't mean you'd sit in it," Finn told him. "I meant that the haggis could form a pyramid up against the side of the tower that we could climb so we could get to the witch's window."

"Oh," Sir Jacobus said, slapping a paw to his forehead. "That makes a lot more sense." He turned to the army of magic haggis. "You need to do what he just said."

CHAPTER 12

The haggis started hopping around at the base of the witch's tower, piling on top of one another. Marceline tried to stop them by throwing boots and candlesticks and other random items, but she only managed to slightly delay the growing pyramid of stomach meat. "What is wrong with you, bringing all these haggis here?" she yelled out the window at Finn and Sir Jacobus. "You can't just introduce a new species to this island. How are these haggis going to affect the natural habitat?"

"She's starting to panic," Finn said gleefully. "In another few minutes we can start climbing. And then the fun begins."

The haggis had a setback when Marceline threw a chair out the window, knocking a bunch of them to the ground, but they simply duplicated themselves and kept building.

"That's it!" the witch bellowed out the window. "I don't know what you think you're doing, but I've had enough." She thrust her arms straight out and then directed them toward the haggis. Bolts of fire flashed out of her fingertips.

The fire braised the haggis flesh, but didn't seem to cause them pain or slow them down at all. "Wow," Sir Jacobus said, sniffing the air. "You can really smell the spices in the organ-meat stuffing."

"Don't be gross, dude," his servant told him.

It was only a few more minutes before the haggis breached the castle window. Marceline was hacking at them with her ax guitar, but there were just too many of them. "Come on," Sir Jacobus said, starting to climb the pyramid of organ meat. "Now's our chance."

"You know," Finn said as he, too, started to scale the sheep stomachs. "We've done a lot of weird stuff while out adventuring, and we've seen a lot of gross stuff, but this really has to be some of the weirdest and grossest."

"Hey," Sir Jacobus chastised him, although secretly shuddering as his foot slipped a little on the slick surface of the stomachs. "Don't be so negative. Haggis is a specialty of the Kingdom of Plaid." A few truly disgusting moments of slimy climbing later and they were at the tower window.

"What do you think you're doing?" Marceline demanded. "There are things like front doors, you know. You could try knocking."

Sir Jacobus leaped fearlessly through the window. While doing so he remembered that he hadn't brought any kind of weapon to battle the witch, but it was too late to worry about small details. "Avast, witch," he shouted, hoping he was using words that sounded courageous and romantic. "Release my lady love and I will consider sparing your life."

"Don't say 'avast' to me. I should be saying 'avast' to you," Marceline told him. "What you are doing is called breaking and entering. And it's illegal. Now take your sheep stomachs and get out of my house or I'm calling the cops!" A few of the haggis plopped onto the floor and paused, awaiting Sir Jacobus's orders.

"What are you talking about?" Finn wanted to know as he, too, climbed through the window. A dozen or so haggis immediately swarmed around his feet.

"I mean you can't just climb into the window of somebody's home and start shouting old-time pirate talk at them," the witch informed them. "And I don't even know what you were thinking bringing all these enchanted sheep stomachs. That's just not sanitary. There is something seriously wrong with you two."

"Don't try to fool us with your tricky witch talk," Finn said. "This is Sir Jacobus Gooddog and I am his loyal servant and best friend Finnish Biped."

Marceline gave them a funny look. "Yeah, I know. We met the other night. Remember?" She folded her arms and glared at them. "Why don't you just tell me why you're here?"

Sir Jacobus stepped forward, clearing his throat. He put a paw to his chest. "I am here to vanquish the witch and free my lady love, who is being held prisoner in the tower. Now, like I said before, avast!"

"Are you calling me a witch?" Marceline asked, looking rather surprised.

"Well, yeah," Finn told her. "You're always wearing black and stuff. And we saw that fire spell shooting out of your fingers."

Marceline rolled her eyes. "I can't believe you two. Just because someone likes to wear black doesn't make them a witch. And even if I was a witch, that doesn't mean I am holding anyone prisoner."

"So . . . you're not a witch?" Sir Jacobus asked. He wondered if he should feel foolish or if this was just one of the witch's tricks.

"No," Marceline snarled. "I'm a Vampire. Thank you for asking. What made you think I was a witch? Besides the fact that black is my favorite color?" Unobserved by anyone, the few haggis that had entered the room appeared to be discussing something. Then, one by one, they quietly slipped out the window.

"Well . . ." Finn dragged his toe along the flagstone floor. "When we first tried to borrow a boat, not a single captain would lend one to us, even though it would be for Sir Jacobus Gooddog."

"I don't blame them," the non-witch said. "I wouldn't lend you a boat, either. Everybody in the Kingdom of Plaid knows what you did to Princess Bubblegum's ice-cream maker when you borrowed that."

"Geez, make it snow vanilla fudge for a few days and nobody ever forgets," Sir Jacobus grumbled.

"Yeah, but then after we special-borrowed a boat, we got attacked by sardines," Finn went on. "Really mean ones. You had to have bewitched those little fish to be so angry."

"Believe it or not, I'm not in charge of the marine life that surrounds this island," Marceline told them, sounding indignant. "Why do you think I fly everywhere? I'm not dealing with those crazy fish."

"Yeah, but when we got here it was all rainy and then Sir Jacobus got a really bad splinter and then there was nothing to eat on the boat that we special-borrowed. So, if you're not a witch, then how do you explain all that?" Finn demanded, still not convinced.

"So you're mad because you took someone's boat without asking and there was no food on it? And the weather was bad and your boss got a splinter? Those are the reasons I'm being accused of witchcraft?"

Marceline couldn't hide her astonishment.

"Okay. A lot of that stuff sounds pretty stupid when you say it out loud," Finn admitted. He was almost convinced, but then he thought of something. "So why were you fighting us, then, if you're not some evil witch?"

CHAPTER 13

"Yeah," Sir Jacobus said. "If you're not a witch then explain why you were fighting us when we were trying to get into this castle."

"Because you were trying to break into my home!" the Vampire yelled at them. "I was just hanging out, looking out the window, when suddenly you two jerks show up and start throwing enchanted sheep stomachs at me. What was I supposed to do? Not fight back?"

"Oh well . . . when you put it that way," Sir Jacobus said, feeling uneasy. "I guess you have a point."

Finn thought of a new argument. "But what about at the ball?"

Marceline gave him a tired look. "What about it? There was some weird competition and then a food fight broke out so we left."

"Yeah, but before that you wouldn't let Lady Rainicorn dance with Sir Jacobus," the Hu-manservant pointed out. "Now that seems like a real witchy thing to do."

"Yeah, why were you being so mean?" Sir Jacobus demanded.

"I wasn't being mean. I was just being a good friend," Marceline insisted. "Lady Rainicorn always has guys hitting on her and a lot of them are real jerks," she said, shooting a significant look in their direction. "She said she'd give me a signal if she actually wanted to dance with a guy and she wasn't giving me the signal."

"Hey, wait a minute." Sir Jacobus folded his arms.

"If you and Lady Rainicorn are such good friends and all, then why do you have her locked in a tower?"

"Yeah," Finn added, folding his arms, too.

"Wow, you two are thick," Marceline told them. She also knew how to fold her arms and she did so to prove it. "I don't have her locked anywhere. We're roommates. This tower is my bedroom and that tower is her bedroom. We're friends. We share the rent. Living in an island fortress is really expensive, in case you couldn't guess."

"I still don't know." Finn was skeptical. Marceline did put up a pretty good argument, but that also might have been a witch trick.

"Oh, for crying out loud," Marceline said, sounding completely exasperated. "I'll just call her in here and prove that she's my roommate and not my prisoner."

Just then Lady Rainicorn entered the room. Her mane swished through the air, and her rainbow skin glistened in the lamp light. "왜 성문 밖에 거대한

더미의 하기스가 있는거죠?" she asked.

The Vampire rolled her eyes. "Yeah, I'd be wondering about the huge pile of haggis outside the castle, too, if I were you. Ask these two ding-dongs," she said.

"어머, 미안해요. 낮잠자느라 손님이 온줄 몰랏어요." Lady Rainicorn turned to greet the visitors.

"Yeah, well, I'm sorry your nap got interrupted, but I wouldn't exactly call these two guests. I think you probably remember Sir Jacobus and Finn from the ball," Marceline said, by way of introduction.

"Duuuuuuuuuurh . . . heh . . . heh . . . ," Sir Jacobus said. The pupils of his eyes were replaced by Valentine's hearts. His own heart started pounding out of his chest like a cuckoo clock.

And Lady Rainicorn in return said, "오 . . . 와 . . ." The pupils of her eyes turned to hearts as well, and her cheeks turned bright pink with the first flush of true love.

"Uh, are you okay?" Marceline asked, full of concern for her roommate.

"그는 제이코버스 구독 선생이에요," Lady Rainicorn said in a fervent whisper. Her voice sounded like tinkling bells to Sir Jacobus's ears. "연회에서 그 남자를 본 이후로 자꾸만 그가 생각나요," she added with a gasp.

"Really?" Marceline asked, doing little to hide her surprise. "You've been thinking of Sir Jacobus ever since the ball? Seriously?"

"I think that's your cue," Finn said, nudging his friend forward.

At first Sir Jacobus was too stunned to speak. But after gathering his wits about him, he managed to approach Lady Rainicorn. "My lady," he said. She extended her hoof and he bestowed on it an admiring kiss. "Woooo. Wooo. Woo. Woooo," he started saying. "Wooo. Woo. Woo. Woooo."

Lady Rainicorn felt her heart beating quickly in

her chest like the wings of a dove when it takes flight. She had greatly admired Sir Jacobus at the ball, but never dreamed that a Gooddog would show the slightest interest in a Rainicorn. Still, she did not understand the weird noise he was making. She wondered if it was a cultural thing. "저 남자 뭐하는거죠?" she whispered to her roommate, an awkward smile pasted on her face for fear of giving offense.

Marceline released a long-suffering sigh. "I really don't know what he's doing. I've been battling these jokers for most of the afternoon."

"Uh, are you okay?" Finn asked his boss, his voice full of concern.

"Yeah, why do you ask?" Sir Jacobus asked, taking a short break from making his woo-woo noise.

"Yeah, well . . . why do you keep making that weird noise?" his Hu-manservant wanted to know. "I think you're kind of weirding the ladies out a little." And himself, too, although he wasn't willing to admit it.

"I'm wooing Lady Rainicorn," Sir Jacobus said, annoyed that he had to explain himself. "Don't you know anything?"

Finn frowned. "Are you sure you're doing it right?"

"Of course I'm sure I'm doing it right," Sir Jacobus said, growing irritated with the interruptions. "How do you think you're supposed to woo a girl?"

"Uh . . . guys?" Marceline said, interrupting them both. "First of all, that's not how you're supposed to woo a girl. But secondly, nobody has time for wooing right now."

"Why not?" Sir Jacobus asked. He was convinced he was wooing correctly, and Lady Rainicorn looked pretty happy.

"Because that giant swarm of haggis you brought here is up to something," she informed them.

CHAPTER 14

Everyone rushed to look out the small tower window. It was true. The haggis were up to something. They had all regrouped on the lawn in front of the castle. They were hopping around and appeared to be whispering to each other and then shooting shifty looks toward the castle tower. "Oh. That can't be good," Sir Jacobus said, slowly shaking his head. He turned to his lady love. "I'm sorry, Lady Rainicorn, but the wooing will have to wait."

"이해해요," said the Rainicorn. The haggis were making everyone nervous.

Sir Jacobus smiled. "I knew you'd understand."

"Where did you get all these sheep stomachs?" Marceline wondered.

"Actually, we just got the one stomach," Finn explained. "But a sorcerer put a spell on it so that when Sir Jacobus said the magic words, it would help us vanquish our enemies. Oh, but he told us not to say the magic words unless we really, really needed the haggis to help because once it got going, it would not stop until we had vanquished you."

"Well, then why did you say the magic words?" the Vampire demanded. "I wasn't doing anything to hurt you."

"Yeah, but we didn't know that at the time," Sir Jacobus told her. "And besides, I wanted to get the whole battle over with so I could start wooing Lady Rainicorn."

"*Grrrr* . . . ," Marceline growled. "I can't believe you unleashed magic haggis on this island without even knowing if we were enemies or not. That was not a smart thing to do."

"Yeah." Sir Jacobus had to agree with her. "I can definitely see that now."

"Why don't you just say the magic words that make the haggis stop?" Marceline suggested.

"Um . . . well . . ." Sir Jacobus scuffed his foot along the stone floor. "You see, we never exactly got to that part."

Both Marceline and Lady Rainicorn stared at him with looks of disbelief painted across their faces. "You mean to tell me, you unleashed a horde of haggis without knowing how to stop them?" the Vampire demanded.

"Yeah . . . that's about the size of it," Sir Jacobus had to admit. All the Vampire could do was shake her head.

"Uh . . . the haggis seem to be making a move," Finn said, sounding rather nervous.

It was true. They had formed a slingshot using

two trees and some stretchy rubber they must have found somewhere. There was a line of stomachs waiting to be shot at the castle. The rest of the haggis started swarming the base of the tower. Then more haggis piled on top of the first group. And then more piled on top of the second group. "They're doing the pyramid maneuver again," Finn exclaimed.

Marceline grabbed her ax guitar and swatted away the first haggis to come sailing in the window via the slingshot. She turned to the untamed scoundrel. "Command them to stop," she said. "If you're the one that got them to start the attack, then you can obviously make them stop. Just stick your head out the window and let them know that the battle is over."

"But the magic guy who made the haggis said once released, the haggis wouldn't stop until my enemies were vanquished," Sir Jacobus explained.

"Well, then stick your head out the window and tell them I'm vanquished," she said, giving him a shove.

"Uh . . . hello? Haggis?" Sir Jacobus began after clearing his throat a few times and shoving his head out the window. "I appreciate what you're doing and all, but the battle is over. The witch has been vanquished, so you don't have to attack the tower anymore or anything." The haggis paid no attention to him.

Marceline joined him in sticking her head out the window. "He's right," she called down to the hundreds of sheep stomachs. "Totally vanquished here. I mean, you've just never seen someone as vanquished as I am right now." The haggis continued to ignore them.

Finn ran up to the window and chucked out a rocking chair. "Hah! Take that, you haggis. That's for not listening," he shouted.

"Hey! That was my grandmother's," Marceline yelled. "You could ask first, you know."

"Sorry," Finn mumbled. "But I saw you throw that chair earlier." He looked down at the haggis.

"Yeah, it didn't really stop them the first time, either."

He was right. The pile of haggis was getting closer and closer to the windowsill.

Finn and Sir Jacobus stood, wide-eyed, completely at a loss. Marceline looked from one to the other, then realized they were not going to be any help. "Okay, fine. We girls will handle this," she said decisively. "Lady, go get that big vat of clotted cream we have in the larder. Finn, you help her. It's going to be heavy. Sir Jacobus"—she shoved the guitar into his hands—"I'm going to start blasting the haggis with fire, but if any of them get past me, you need to hit them back out the window."

"Got it," Sir Jacobus told her. Everyone immediately scrambled to their tasks.

"We are totally vanquished here," the Vampire said as she straightened her arms and blasted the haggis pyramid with a few bolts of fire. "You're wasting your time attacking us because we've already been vanquished," she said, zapping them again for good measure.

"It's no use," Sir Jacobus said, smacking a haggis with the guitar as soon as it bounced through the window, making it bounce back out again. "What do you think they'll do once they get in here?"

"Isn't that something you should have asked when you got the magic haggis in the first place?" Marceline shouted, zapping the mound of stomachs with another blast of fire. Sir Jacobus was at a loss as to what to say.

"우리 클로티드 크림 있어요," Lady Rainicorn said as she and Finn shoved a huge iron cauldron into the room.

"Yeah, and it's superheavy," Finn added. "What's wrong with this cream, anyway?" he asked, poking at the white, fluffy stuff. "It's all thick and weird and stuff."

"It's clotted cream, you ding-dong," Marceline

snarled. "You have to have seen it before; it's a specialty of the Kingdom of Plaid."

"Never heard of it," Finn told her, flicking a glob of the thick cream back into the vat.

Sir Jacobus shot his friend a seriously annoyed look. "Do you even live in this kingdom?"

Finn shrugged. "I thought I did."

The haggis were nearly at the windowsill.

"It doesn't matter!" Marceline shouted. "Put the cauldron right up to the window," she ordered. Once the cauldron was in place, she said, "Okay, now everyone gather round." The army of haggis was very close to breaching the castle. "On the count of three we're going to pour the cream onto the haggis." Everyone positioned themselves around the large iron cauldron. It looked quite heavy. "Ready? One. Two. Three!" Everyone heaved, tipping the large vat at an extreme angle, but nothing came out.

"It's too thick!" Sir Jacobus exclaimed.

"그 기타 도끼를 써요," Lady Rainicorn suggested. "저것으로 파내어요."

Sir Jacobus applied the ax guitar and was able splash large dollops of the thick cream onto the invading haggis. Each time a bit of the clotted cream touched one of the sheep stomachs, it went *pop* like a soap bubble and was gone, leaving only a little blue mist that vanished in the wind.

"It's working!" Sir Jacobus shouted. He kept flinging the cream, and more haggis kept quickly disappearing. *Pop, pop, pop, pop, pop.*

"Keep slinging that clotted cream," Marceline told the Gooddog. "It's working! It's working!"

Finally, there was just one haggis left. The sheep stomach looked almost forlorn all by itself. "I think that might be the first one," Finn said. "The original one we got from the magic butcher."

"You're probably right," Sir Jacobus said, splattering it with a heavy coating of clotted cream.

If a sheep stomach could sigh, then that's what it did. The haggis took a few hops back toward the boat, then disappeared in a dazzling display of blue sparkles.

"Okay, well, that's over with," Finn said, brushing his hands together to brush off some dirt. "Say, why did you two have a big vat of clotted cream, anyway?" he asked, turning to Marceline.

The Vampire shrugged. "It's the only way to get rid of an army of magical haggis."

"Okay," Sir Jacobus said. "My enemy is vanquished." Marceline glared at him so he quickly added, "So to speak. Wasn't it Lincoln who said 'the best way to get rid of an enemy is to make them a friend' or something like that?" The Vampire just rolled her eyes, so the Gooddog continued. "Now that we got those pesky haggis out of the way, I can return to my wooing."

"Not more wooo, woo, woo," Finn said, slapping a hand over his eyes and shaking his head.

"No, I have a better idea," Sir Jacobus told him. Stepping forward, he swept Lady Rainicorn into his muscular arms and said, "Lady Rainicorn, I have been willingly disowned by my family because I wanted to be with you. When I first saw you at the ball, I realized you were the most beautiful creature I'd ever seen. I came here today to ask you to be my one and only."

"아," Lady Rainicorn gasped, feeling a bit lightheaded by his manly manliness. "그대를 처음본 이후로 단 한번도 그대를 잊어본적이 없어요. 물론이죠, 난 그대에게 단 하나밖에 없는 사람이 돼고 싶어요."

"You've thought of nothing but me since the ball? Seriously? And you're willing to be my one and only? That's great," Sir Jacobus Gooddog said, bestowing on her a passionate kiss. "But I feel I should warn you. Even though we will be together, we can never get married."

"왜 안돼죠?" Lady Rainicorn asked, sounding a bit disappointed.

"Because I will always be," he said, drawing a deep breath and placing a paw over his heart, "an untamed scoundrel."

Lady Rainicorn blinked at him with her large, beautiful eyes. "나 결혼하고 싶어요," she told him.

"Okay," Sir Jacobus said with a shrug. "If that's what you want to do, let's get married then."

Lady Rainicorn and the untamed scoundrel lived happily ever after.

THE END

AND NOW . . .
here's an epic excerpt from:

Epic Tales from

ADVENTURE TIME™

Queen of Rogues

by T. T. MacDangereuse

CHAPTER 1

Fionna's sweaty palms dampened her skirt as she lifted its hem and stepped onto the gangplank leading up to P. Gumball's massive yacht. She tried to focus on the ship's deck, just ten feet away, and on the laughter and music the wind carried to her ears. Just ten feet and she'd . . .

Be on a ship. Which was about to set sail. On the ocean.

Fear washed over her and she froze. She couldn't stop looking at the water, imagining the creatures lurking beneath its mercurial surface. Creatures with tentacles, spines, teeth as long as her arm, creatures that would be able to get her if she fell in. All it would take was a single misstep on that thin, slick plank . . . She shuddered. Despite her best intentions, Fionna's thalassophobia was getting the better of her.

"Glob, what's the problem?" Lumpy Space Prince whined. He tugged at her hand as he bobbed in the air beside her. "You wanted to go to this stupid party, so, like, let's get going."

Sweat stood out on Fionna's forehead. She licked her lips as a paper streamer floated past her. "I . . . I dunno. Maybe this wasn't such a good idea."

Lumpy Space Prince heaved a sigh that was overly dramatic, even for him, and folded his arms across his chubby chest. "This is so like you, Fionna. You drag me here all the way from Lumpy Space for this lumping party, and now you don't even want to go? Like, I totally should have expected this. You're the worst pretend girlfriend ever."

Fionna swallowed. She did want to go to the party.
She'd been so excited when she and her roommate,
Cake the Cat, had received their invitations just two
days ago. The invites, pressed onto glittering sheets of
ruby-red Candy cardstock, had been hand-delivered
by a sharply attired Green Gumdrop. Fionna had
been too shocked to say thank you as the Gumdrop
tipped his bowler hat and took his leave.

"Actual invitations!" Cake had exclaimed. "Hon,
that's incredible!" Her tail fuzzed with excitement.
P. Gumball's parties were infamous. "And we each
get to bring a plus one! I know who I'm asking—Lord
Monochromicorn!"

Fionna's heart fluttered. P. Gumball was a famous
recluse—everyone in Candy Kingdom had a fanciful
story they'd heard from the son of an aunt of a brother
of a sister of a father of a mouse, but who knew if any
of those stories were true? According to the gossip
she'd heard, Gumball was simultaneously ten feet tall,

a half-orc, a ghost, and a werewolf. She'd heard that he had earned his wealth through mysterious, unsavory means involving demons and the Nightosphere; by falling into a sinkhole and discovering an enormous cache of diamonds; by keeping a herd of captive rainicorns who wept tears of pure gold; through an inheritance left to him by a kindly great-great-great-grandfather who had died of natural causes at the ripe old age of six hundred and five.

Fionna was no fool—she knew most everything was probably nonsense, but that only heightened her curiosity. And now she'd finally been given a chance to attend one of his parties, to meet the mysterious millionaire himself. She wasn't about to let a fear of the ocean get in the way of that.

Or so she'd told herself.

The wind picked up, luffing the yacht's sails, rocking the gangplank beneath Fionna's feet. Her stomach quivered. She swallowed hard and, struggling to calm herself, focused on the letters painted in gold on the ship's hull: *The Banoffee.* Glob, what kind of a name was that?

"Fionna! What the lump? Like, come on!"

Lumpy Space Prince was moments away from sinking into a good long pout, she realized. She struggled to hide her annoyance. He hadn't wanted to go, and she hadn't wanted to invite him, but everyone else had already paired up. She'd been determined not to be the only person without a plus one.

"A-all right." Lumpy Space Prince was right. They were already late. Cake had left hours ago, astride Lord Monochromicorn's rippling back. Taking a deep breath, she closed her eyes, dashed up the gangplank, and leaped onto the deck.

About the Author

The elusive T. T. MacDangereuse is one of the most popular authors in all of Ooo. Although little is known about her private life, it is rumored that she learned the art of storyship at a very young age after being rescued from a pack of jitter-bugging party bears by The Prince of the Pencil Kingdom. She claims that all her story ideas are inspired hallucinations caused by eating too many apple pies.